The First Gift of Christmas

written by
William A. Guiffré

illustrated by
Cheri Ann Baron

And it came to pass while they were there, that the days for her to be delivered were fulfilled. And she brought forth her firstborn son, and wrapped him in swaddling clothes, and laid him in the manger, because there was no room for them in the inn.

Luke 2:6-7

Coastal Publishing, Inc.
504 Amberjack Way
Summerville, SC 29485
1-843-821-6168
coastalpublishing@earthlink.net
www.coastalpublishingbooks.com

Publisher's Cataloging-in-Publication Data

Guiffré, William A. 1934-
The first gift of Christmas / written by William A.
Guiffré ; illustrated by Cheri Ann Baron.
p. cm.
SUMMARY: A story about the birth of Jesus from the viewpoint
of the innkeeper's son, David, whose unselfish gift of love marks a
turning point for everyone in David's family.

Audience: Grades K-8

ISBN 1-931650-21-7 - HB

ISBN 1-931650-33-0 - PB

1. Jesus Christ--Nativity--Juvenile fiction.
[1. Jesus Christ--Nativity--Fiction. 2. Christmas--Fiction.]
I. Baron, Cheri Ann. II. Title.

PZ7.G985Fi 2002   [E]

QBI33-1016

An enchanting parable about a blanket that makes its way in and out of the life of Jesus. Like the wonderful story about the fourth wise man, this fictional story conveys a reminder that the life of Jesus impacted many more people and events then were recorded in the Bible or are handed down to us by oral tradition. With little children we can only imagine who some of those people were and what those events might have been.
The Most Rev. Robert J. Baker, S.T.D. Bishop Diocese of Charleston, SC

I am grateful to have had the opportunity to review The First Gift of Christmas. William Guiffre has told a very creative story that speaks both to a child's security attachment to a blanket, youthful altruism that grows into generosity of spirit, and the healing force of that good will. The way he blends Christmas and Easter is profoundly constructive, though Catholic Christians will recognize Veronica far more readily than will Protestants. Veronica is known predominantly through the Stations of the Cross, a tradition kept by Roman Catholics and some High Church Anglicans but not by those of the left wing of the Reformation (like us Baptists!). The illustrations are very effective, colorful and bright with detail. Young readers will find this book very attractive as will parents who read to their children as a way of sharing the faith. Of course as a member of the emergency services community, I am deeply grateful for the dedication.
The Reverend Dr. W. Kenneth Williams, Pastor First Baptist Church of Rochester, NY

The First Gift of Christmas is a Christian story translated for the young. It takes the wonderful Christmas story and gives it another view from that of a young boy. Many children have a favorite toy or blanket that they have had from infancy and so it is easy for them to relate to David and his blanket. William Guiffre takes the Christmas story a step further in detailing what happens with the blanket after the Holy Family leaves the manger and continues on their journey. It is a story that teaches sharing, giving and loving in a gentle way that a young child can understand. This book would be suitable for any young child and it would be most appropriate at Christmas time when wanting and sharing gifts is sometimes difficult for youngsters. I would highly recommend this beautiful book.
The Reverend Matthew H. Clark, Bishop Diocese of Rochester, NY

Dr William Guiffré
Author

Following graduation from the University of Rochester, Dr William Guiffré served in the U.S. Navy for three years and returned to Upstate New York where he became an English teacher at Brighton Junior High School.

In addition to teaching, his career in public education included ten years as a guidance counselor and nineteen as an administrator, the last fifteen of which he served as high school principal in Victor, New York. After one year of retirement, he returned to serve for six years on the Victor Board of Education.

Dr. Guiffré resides with his wife Ann on Kiawah Island, South Carolina but returns to summer in Inlet, New York in the Adirondack Mountains where they can be closer to their seven children and their twenty-three grandchildren who have been the inspiration for him to write picture books for children.

Dedication - This book is about a gift given in love. I am honored to dedicate it to all those career and volunteer emergency personnel who each day offer their lives as a gift for others.

Foreword - David's gift of love to the Baby Jesus becomes a turning point for everyone in David's family.

Illustrator - Cheri Baron first worked as an artist in her hometown of Leominster, Massachusetts. Her parents encouraged her talent with studio art classes, and plenty of paper and paints. She attended Salem State College and became an art teacher. Newly married she moved to Milwaukee, Wisconsin where she did a series of watercolor paintings. Now Cheri's home is the Hudson River Valley in New York. Her husband Danny is a New York City firefighter. She keeps busy homeschooling their children, Alyssa and Kelsey. Cheri enjoys hiking and camping with her family. She believes that each moment they have together is a gift, and she is grateful for it.

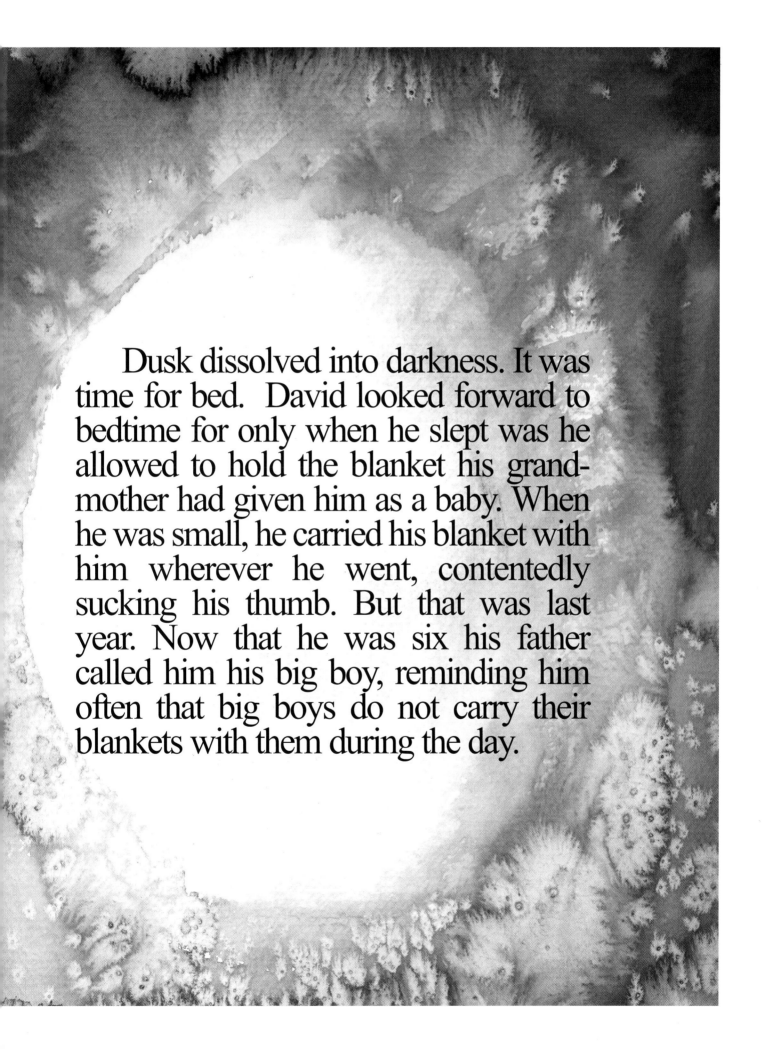

Dusk dissolved into darkness. It was time for bed. David looked forward to bedtime for only when he slept was he allowed to hold the blanket his grandmother had given him as a baby. When he was small, he carried his blanket with him wherever he went, contentedly sucking his thumb. But that was last year. Now that he was six his father called him his big boy, reminding him often that big boys do not carry their blankets with them during the day.

David loved his father very much. For the past month though, David had seen his father looking sad and worried.

Ever since his sister was born she and David's mother had not been well. Each day they both seemed weaker and weaker.

As he knelt by his bed to ask God to help them, David could see the bright new star through his window. He had seen many stars before but none had been as bright nor stayed so directly overhead.

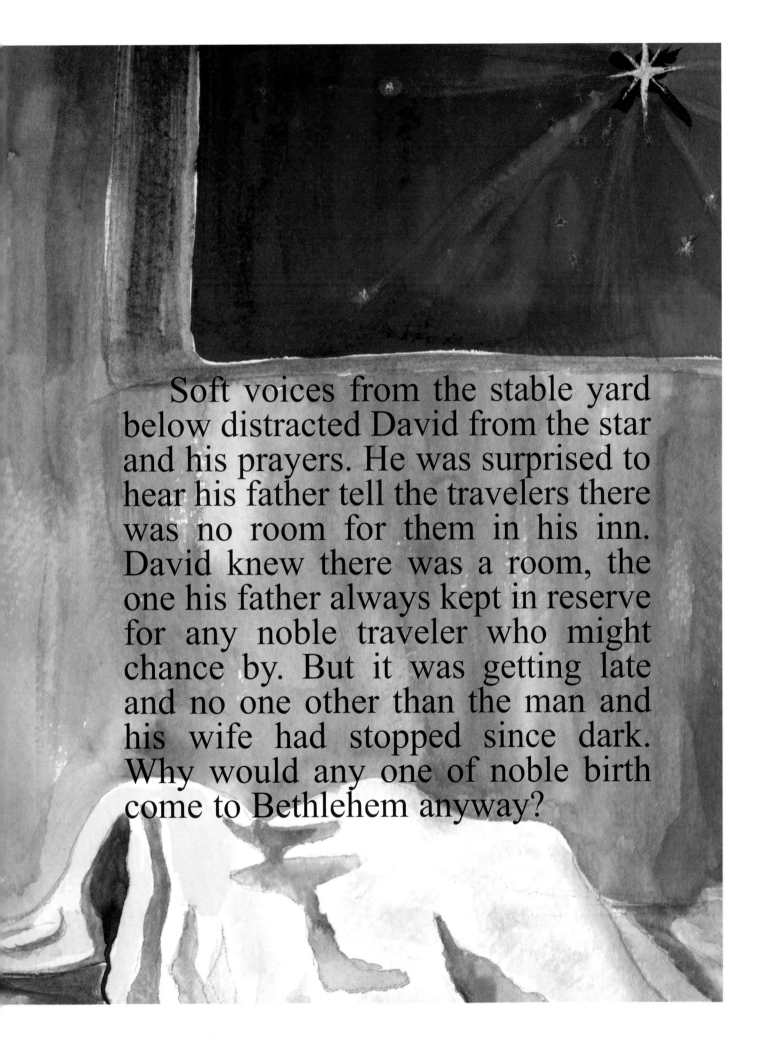

Soft voices from the stable yard below distracted David from the star and his prayers. He was surprised to hear his father tell the travelers there was no room for them in his inn. David knew there was a room, the one his father always kept in reserve for any noble traveler who might chance by. But it was getting late and no one other than the man and his wife had stopped since dark. Why would any one of noble birth come to Bethlehem anyway?

Curious, David left his bed and approached his window. If he stretched as far as he could, stood on tip toes, and then stretched a little bit more, he could see the travelers his father had sent to the stable to sleep. They were both weary and the woman looked just like his mother did the day she gave birth to his sister. He could not stop thinking how cold the clear night air was and how worried the husband looked.

Too troubled to sleep, he exclaimed outloud, "I must go see if I can get them something. I know mother would have found bread for them to eat and she would have asked father to allow them to stay in the royal room too."

Determined to do something, David left his room and went to the stable.

The night was still and the stars danced to unheard music. All nature held its breath as from the stable came the cry of the newborn child. The sound reminded David of his lambs and how they shivered when first born. If they were cold, then this baby would freeze without a warm cover. He raced to his room and back to the stable, bringing with him his most treasured possession, his blanket.

Shyly he approached and offered it to the father.

"Mary, this young lad has brought Jesus his first gift."

With a smile and a gentle, "thank you", she took the blanket and wrapped the baby snugly.

"Your blanket is special to you, isn't it?"

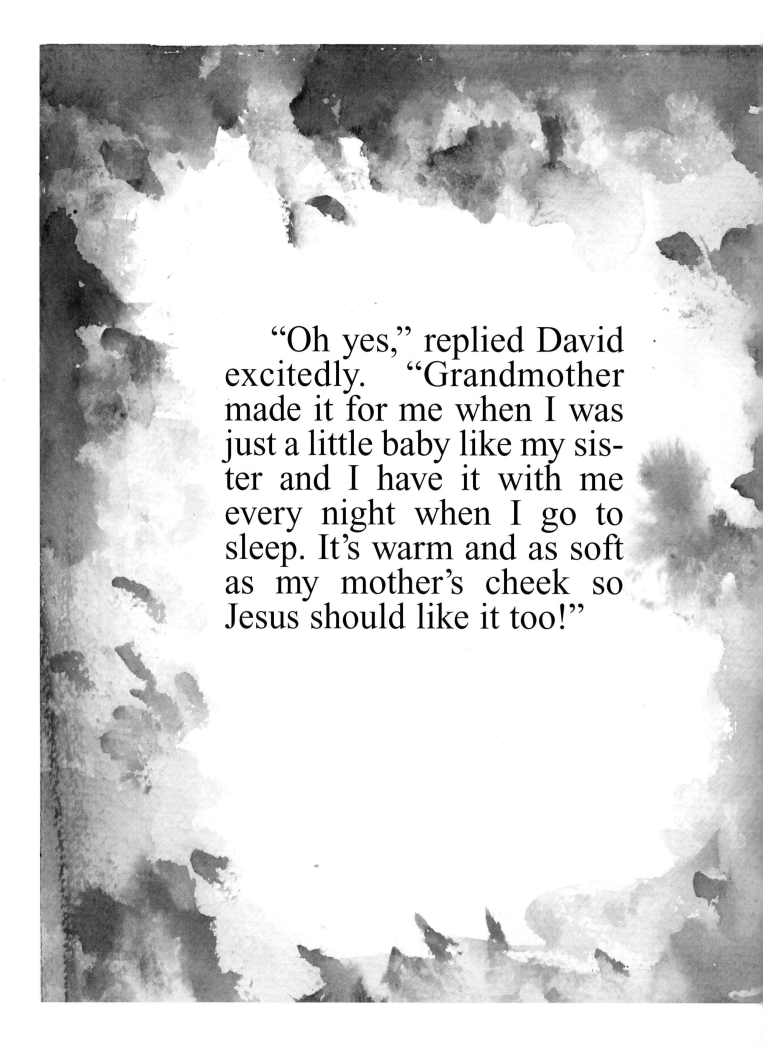

"Oh yes," replied David excitedly. "Grandmother made it for me when I was just a little baby like my sister and I have it with me every night when I go to sleep. It's warm and as soft as my mother's cheek so Jesus should like it too!"

"I am sure he will, for your gift has been given in love to God's little one. Jesus will sleep well tonight."

When he returned to his bed, David slept without his blanket for the very first time.

Never had he slept better!

Several days later when Joseph, Mary and the baby Jesus were about to resume their journey, David came to say goodbye to his new friends. As he approached, Mary removed the blanket from Jesus and returned it to David.

"Sharing your blanket with Jesus will never be forgotten. Perhaps now you will share it with someone else who needs to be touched by your love just as we have been."

As David watched them disappear over the hills, he knew he would never forget them. He knew also he would no longer need his blanket. Mary was right; his sister could use it.

Quietly he entered his mother's darkened room and placed the blanket still warmed by Jesus's touch over Veronica's frail body.

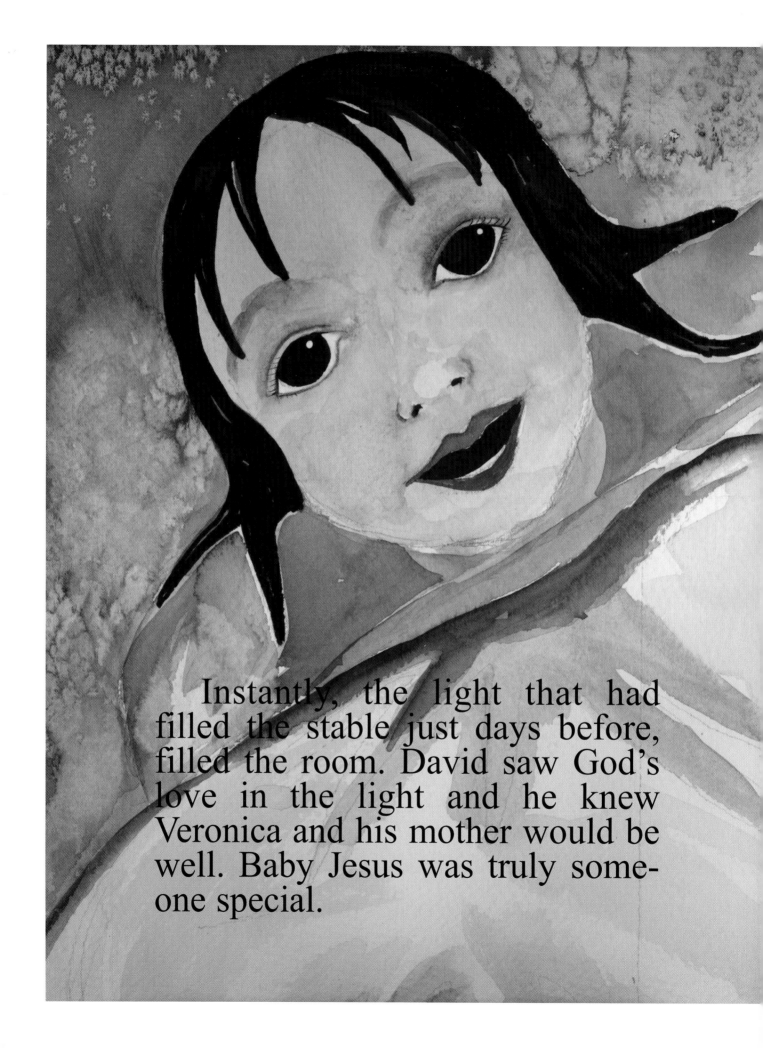

Instantly, the light that had filled the stable just days before, filled the room. David saw God's love in the light and he knew Veronica and his mother would be well. Baby Jesus was truly some-one special.

From then on, Veronica never parted with her special blanket until that day, years later, when she met Jesus carrying his cross to his crucifixion and she wiped his face to clear the blood and perspiration. There, on the blanket that had first warmed his body, Jesus left the image of his sacred face.

The first gift of Christmas had become the first gift of Easter.

The story of Veronica's veil has been part of Christian tradition for nearly 2000 years. It has been commemorated in numerous paintings as well as in early Christian literature.

The End
and
The Beginning

Other titles written by
William A. Guiffré:

Gramma's Glasses
The Wrong Side of the Bed
Angelita's Song